All We Need of Hell

Also by Rika Lesser

Poetry

    Etruscan Things, 1983

Poetry in Translation

    Holding Out (Poems of Rainer Maria Rilke), 1975

    Hours in the Garden and Other Poems by Hermann Hesse, 1978

    Guide to the Underworld by Gunnar Ekelöf, 1980

    Rilke: Between Roots, 1986

    A Child Is Not a Knife: Selected Poems of Göran Sonnevi, 1993

Retellings for Children

    Hansel and Gretel (Illustrated by Paul O. Zelinsky), 1984

    My Sister Lotta and Me (Pictures by Charlotte Ramel), 1993

ALL WE NEED OF HELL

Poems by Rika Lesser

University of North Texas Press
Denton, Texas

August '95

For Richard,
After all these years . . . .
Let's try for knowledge of heaven
next time around. With love,
R.

First Edition 1995

10   9   8   7   6   5   4   3   2   1

Permissions
University of North Texas Press
P. O. Box 13856
Denton, TX 76203

The paper used in this book meets the minimum requirements of the
American National Standard for Permanence of Paper for Printed Library
Materials, z39.48.1984. Binding materials have been chosen for durability.

Library of Congress Cataloging-in-Publication Data

Lesser, Rika.
All we need of hell : poems / by Rika Lesser.
p.   cm.
ISBN 0-929398-85-8 (cloth) : — ISBN 0-929398-92-0 (pbk.)
1. Manic-depressive psychoses—Poetry.   2. Women—Psychology—
Poetry.   I. Title.
PS3562.E837A45   1995
811'.54—dc20   94-40015
                                       CIP

The lines of Homer embedded in the poem "Nepenthe" are from *The
Odyssey*, translated by Robert Fitzgerald. Copyright © 1961, 1963 by Robert
Fitzgerald, renewed 1989 by Benedict R. L. Fitzgerald, on behalf of the
Fitzgerald Children.

Cover oil painting by Lena Cronqvist
Cover design by Amy Layton

Acknowledgments

Grateful acknowledgment is made to the following publications, where these poems—sometimes in different form—first appeared:

American Review: "The Room" and "Departures"
Art & Understanding: "BLACK STONES IX: (And I, and Silence)"
Caprice: "A Valediction: Forbidding Moving"
The G. W. Review: "For the Record" and "Shocking Treatment"
Hubbub: "BLACK STONES V: (From One to Another)"
        "BLACK STONES VII: (Others, Can wrestle—)"
        "BLACK STONES VIII: (And were You lost, I would be—)"
NER/BLQ (*New England Review and Bread Loaf Quarterly*): "The Second
        Time" and "Other Lives"
New Virginia Review: "BLACK STONES XIII: (As light)"
1990 Quarterly: "BLACK STONES VI: (Falling)"
The Paris Review: "Epilogue: *Dödsdansen*"
Partisan Review: "Love"
Pequod: "Escape Attempt" and "Life: It Must Suffice Us"
Ploughshares: "BLACK STONES I / II / III " and "Matthew's Passion"
Southwest Review: "The Other Life"
Western Humanities Review: "On Lithium: After One Year / After Two /
        The Third Year"
"Nepenthe" first appeared in *Celebrating Women: Twenty Years of
        Coeducation at Yale College, The Commemorative Journal*, 1990,
        edited by Alison Buttenheim.
"Shocking Treatment" was reprinted in *Articulations: The Body and Illness in
        Poetry*, University of Iowa Press, 1994, edited by Jon Mukand.

Lena Cronqvist's oil painting, *Upplevelserna målas över* ("The Experiences Being Painted Over"), which appears on the cover of *All We Need of Hell*, dates from 1971 and measures 120 x 136 cm. I am indebted to her for allowing me to use it in connection with this book.

I also wish to thank many a dear friend—too many to name—and especially the members of my family for their patience, fortitude, support, and for their love.

For Julie Low
who helped bring me back to life

and in memory of Matthew Ward
who showed me how precious it is

My life closed twice before its close—
It yet remains to see
If Immortality unveil
A third event to me

So huge, so hopeless to conceive
As these that twice befell.
Parting is all we know of heaven,
And all we need of hell.

—Emily Dickinson

Contents

I

II

III

IV

I

The Room

In the room that's known no fire in seven years
I build one, strike a match; it seems more real
to me in Swedish: *en tändsticka*, a tinder
stick, watch the blue walls behind the cigarette's
blue smoke, uninhaled, and the spent gray (there is
ash gray in these ice blue walls) cast their nets.
On the desk, a still life: teapot and strawberry
cheesecake. Wanting coral ceiling, yellow walls.

The room is always as I left it:
furniture, few possessions, new stacks
of junk mail from the months away. How
did I choose the draperies, the bedspread,
with their kellies, turquoises, umbers on
white? What flowers were ever like these?
On the dresser, a bowl of fresh-cut,
maroon chrysanthemums is glaring.
November. Outside the white window
maple leaves still cling. In Brooklyn, things
hold on longer.

I remember the night the room flared from
the orange carpet to one of the beds
with its yellow sheet: a cheesecake iced
with flaming clothes! Leaving my own white room
for the smoke-filled hall that smelled like dinner
(how we mistake the actual for the known),
I called to my heedless sister in the guest room,
"Fran, get off the phone; your room's on fire!"
Tumbling downstairs. Outside the lightly
falling snow. February. The blue room
is always February.

We kept our lives and, for the first days, strength.
Only two ceilings crumbled from the rot
of heavy water. The eyes of the house, upstairs,
knocked out, boarded up. Fran and I slept
downstairs, in the living room. In the basement
our parents. What floor-sweeping demons there were
entered my mother. She came from herself.

What Lares and Penates lurked, abandoned
her. Perhaps the scrolls in the mezuzas burned.
The eyes of the house, knocked out, boarded up.
Each day she wept, as if blind with cataract.

We were under-insured, that is, too
self-assured, but came out all right, got
to buy new clothes, clean of smoke, and went
on going to school, were precocious,
bratty. Fran said I sat up in my sleep
speaking of certain plants sopranos
ate. We talked; we shared no secret
language. "Braint plants . . . " *Burnt* ones? *Brained*?

The months went by. Depressions, doctors, drugs,
shock treatment, love. (How is it that a house
takes hold of you? Why do I dream of theaters,
opera houses? Who are these stunned and gaping
elderly people?) *Hon var ifrån sig*, she came
from herself. Got "well."
                      I think, when I'm
home for a visit, she opens the door
to my room to see if her memory
of me holds on. She keeps the house. Protects
each room. Or do they own her?

Phantastes, Eumnestes, Nameless One who holds
the Present. I must be Anamnestes who
calls to mind again, retrieves. She is Alma.
For a time, she is with us again. This Thanks-
giving. Now I leave, don't like to travel, though
I need to be in new places. In each room
I set books and yellow roses. I try to
keep my house within my head. It is enough
that the heart operates the rest of the body.
I recall only blueprints, monuments,
architectural dreams.

1974

A Question of Belief

The first time wasn't real, I mean
for real, a real attempt. No one
believed me when I said the medicine
was at fault, kept me from sleeping,
thinking, set my limbs tingling. Taking
those pills, staying in that house—
pigeons roosting on the roof, their
insistent coos and cries—in one of my
old bedrooms, made me an invalid.
What they believed was what I said
in scorn, in response to threats. That I'd
like to jump out a window. All I wanted
was sleep.

And in the hospital that first time,
after the countless pills, the ipecac,
the papers signed, the break
with my first shrink, once I had slept
my fill and felt like a child in some
giant's grip, they handed me nearly
the same damned drugs. Again I flipped,
stopped sleeping, believed they would kill me
on Walpurgis Night, not one swift scalpel,
ritual sacrifice—not just the staff,
the other patients too . . .

> *We were so frail. No one*
> *believed what we said.*
> *And we learned to get out*
> *by saying: We won't try it*
> *again. Grateful to be alive,*
> *we will pay our dues. Just*
> *show us the way out of Hell,*
> *dear Doctors, release us. Please.*

For the Record

Death's not a lover, only a release
from the mind spinning its own wheels, a ditch
you could jump into, lie down in for good.
Death's not a lover, just a last resort.

I wanted to talk about memory:
what goes, what stays. Of how, when "psychotic,"
life, events—even in the uneventful
hospital (save a suicide out a high,
sealed window, smashed with a pool cue)—went
by like dreams. Fast, too fast to record.
How I searched the grain of the drawing
paper for figures, traced untold tiny
women and men in unspeakable
postures. How I tore around, in pencil
drew swastikas between the bathroom tiles,
tore open my roommate's treasure chest
of sweets, took candied violets, pastilles,
chocolates, ate some, hurled the rest. Tore back
down the hall with the little woman
shadowing me (I was on C.O.). We
passed a mural, a Brooklyn Prospect former
patients had done: a clock, a statue—
I can't remember more—each painted thing
pointed to my death: that night when I'd be
violated, burned (with cigarettes),
pissed and shat on by the other patients,
then slowly carved with knives. That night. The eve
of May the first. Here is the record:

Between 4/27/85
and 5/2/85 patient was placed
on Constant Observation due to
suicidal ideation with a definite
intent and plan. She also became
paranoid, thinking that people were
going to harm her. On 4/29/85
she was started on Navane 5 mg BID.
Paranoid ideation diminished
rapidly and Navane was gradually
decreased then and discontinued
on 5/12/85.

I was not "suicidal." Had no "intent,"
no "plan." I recall wanting, trying to
escape those who would kill me. I would have
torn a hole in the end of the corridor,
its barred and bolted door. . . .

But to get back to those records. Or those
who keep them. There's so much the Clinical
Perspective fails to take into account!
Would "trained observers" be different if they'd
had a break? Made an attempt?
                              The Head
of Psychiatry grilled me in his office,
"Surely, Miss Lesser, at your age, you have
some view of the afterlife?" I would not
oblige him, admit that my aim or end.
We finish here, I said, and no, I heard
no voices then or at any time.
                              Sometimes,
Good Doctor, I forget you are trained,
not bred, to your calling and speak to you
as if you could *feel* my side. Sometimes,
all over your face I see: That's nuts, maybe
we should increase the medication.
Even now, three years later, as I
docilely swallow three lithium
capsules daily, calling them vitamins,
taking them for fear they keep me sane,
I can't help but remember I never
fully went off the deep end until
a doctor put me on Elavil. . . .
Oh yes, you've said, sometimes when a patient
is depressed—a Manic Depressive II—
and given tricyclic antidepressants,
she will flip over into mania;
the medication only proves the point. . . .
If this is so, then why did it go
unnoticed? Why did I have to lose
two years of my life?
                              My distrust, you know,
is not of lithium, nor solely due
to this episode. There's a history
with my mother in the center. And
now, released from twenty years of drugs
that threatened her health, she is finally
"well."

        Well, at Rockvale they sought to impose
her history on me. Or were they
"flipping me over" deliberately?
Sounding out a hypothesis? (I was
discharged a *classic* Manic Depressive.)
We all were so doped up there, glazed, controlled.
We stared past everyone. And our eyeballs shone.

BLACK STONES   I

It is Thursday, raining
You ask me a question   I
try to answer quickly
definitively or thought-
fully for truly I
do not know
             I go off to
think—but nothing answers—
so hard so long I lose sight

And you who asked are no
longer there   Or you are—though
not as the person who
asked the question   Only as
a mask or a mirror
someone some thing without Life

Answer me, Death Mask, I
have a question!
             Through the holes:
feeble breathing, a faint
gleam where the eyes go   Silence

                    And the masks of those I loved
                    answer solely from their love
                    which seeks to heal, but kills

BLACK STONES   II

You did not want to leave
and so you left
You did not want to cling
but had to hold on
You did not know that time
would ever heal
So you waited waited long
for your heart which might
never again respond
to what it once loved

You could not sleep
but lay down in bed each night
You did not want to eat
but ate to keep yourself well
You could barely speak
others tried to speak for you
You were paralyzed
so they pushed you along
from nowhere to nowhere
And this long stasis
some say is like Death
might in fact be prologue
to something still worse
or better
       Can one turn
around quickly, spin
so quickly as to effect
a miraculous change?

BLACK STONES   III

You speak of change
as if it were something
tangible, something you
wanted, of that final
change which brings peace
Nothing but water and
sleep, drifting from one to
the other   Nothing could
be simpler

          Outside your
dark window lights are lit:
in the street, over doorways,
in windows   Inside each
habitation Life goes
on   In agitation hope
fear   Music is playing
Baths are being run

You speak of change
as if it were something
you desperately wanted
rather than something you
slowly needed
to accomplish

The Second Time

You must put the deed
behind you, as if
it never happened,
or happened to some-
body else. As if
it were not you.

But I remember it so
precisely—I took notes! I
opened the futon bed—or
was it already open,
unmade from the night before?
The rainbow sheets were on, a
blue and white flowered duvet
cover on the blanket. It
was March and cold. I know I
wore my white, bulky, English
sweater, I know by the next
morning's evidence: clothes all
over the floor, pink-orange
splotches over them and on
the blanket, also scattered
on pages of my journal
from that time. Some pills were perched
on a bookshelf; others flew
out of the medicine chest:
  Motrin, Halofed, Dalmane,
  Chlor–Trimeton, lithium.
I started with what was left
of the Noilly Prat, listed
the pills, for each one I took
I recorded a stroke, moved
on to vodka, smiling and
crying, writing—oh, no, I
prefer not to quote. All night
long I threw up, I wiped up
the floor when I failed to reach
the bathroom in time. Waking,
my first groggy thought was: *O-*
kay, Rika, time
to get back to work.

12

*Did you even once
realize the danger
you were in?*

It was not danger I was
aware of but distress. I
feared this attempt would fail. I'd
pondered other means: the leap
from the roof, out the window,
electrifying the bath,
knives, Drano, gas, or lunging
in front of a train. I was
afraid of being alive
and maimed. And yet that day I
wrote: "I'd like the pleasure
of a painful death. I
imagine my mother
weeping over my body.
My father nervously
turning away."
              Danger? With
Crusoe I could say (*after*
he'd seen the cannibals): "I
                     *was as happy in not knowing
my danger as if I had never
really been exposed to it.*"

On Lithium

After One Year

No, I don't seem to have many side
effects: my hands imperceptibly
tremble, and it's damned hard to lose weight.
Though I appear to have more staying
power now, it's not the same. I used
to work in a tunnel, a charged field
at my desk; now the work—translating
Swedish fiction—is just a series
of tasks, queries and replies. Today
I called a German friend in D.C.,
hoping through him to find a British
chemist, all to check one word. And that
word was in English! (We did succeed.)
The *tasks* of the translator, plural,
not Benjamin's singular essay,
the daily grueling *tasks*.

                  Once I worked—
especially that summer in Finland—
ten or more hours a day. Up at
seven, breakfast prepared by a friend,
Hufvudstadsbladet, a second pot
of coffee, and I'd read books, take notes,
translate a bit—chunks of a long poem
by Enckell, read some more, write letters,
be curt on the phone if disturbed (my
friends understood), pick wildflowers,
key them out, see people now and then,
teach English to Chinese scientists,
stoke up the sauna to one hundred
Celsius . . .

          There was a shimmer
on everything. Each day shone like an
ammonite split and polished, nights like
obsidian. Even stormy days,
when I watched the layers of clouds, of
variegated grays, parade past
my windows, douse my balcony . . . No,

things are just not the same. The lightness
and speed are gone, the certainty too.
My nights and days are one. . . . Indifferent
effects of the lithium?

After Two

My hair is thinning, so far all in
one spot, at the nape of my neck, not
visible, thus still tolerable.
The cause may not be known. Hormonal
change is possible. But the redness
and bumps on my scalp that cortisone
won't clear point to lithium. Always
secretly vain about my hair, I
might prefer madness to baldness.
For

the kind I had wasn't all that bad.
Lifelong I suffered periods of
intensive work. Not always as "high"
as in Helsinki in '84
but reliably energetic.
I'd write myself into a state where
nothing but the work mattered, nothing
else existed in fact. Not heaven
exactly; still, somewhere I was calm,
oblivious of my surroundings,
of the world. A place from which all pain
was not simply shut out, but exiled.

Whither has it fled? *Wohin? Wohin?*

At present, I really can't complain.
I'm more disciplined—wake up, shower,
make coffee, work on these "crazy" poems.
But now I'm aware: of the black man
who spends his day on the steps of two
brownstones across the street, of the hum
of Astrid (my AT) or the whir
of the fan, of fire trucks, piercing scents . . .
and Music—once my constant working
companion—can't be put on, demands
all my attention. And now, too, there's
Pain, old friend, old foe, yes, Pain is here.

Events come back, flood over me as
before. What if the memories stayed
and the present vanished?

                    Just last year,
when I tried to work on these poems, I'd
fall asleep. Was I still too depressed?
The wounds too raw? Now I go on for
hours. Surely this means I've improved,
but am I better than *before*?
                         Time
and again I tell myself: Why, sure;
now you are steadier, rarely have
outbursts or fits—"violent mood swings"
describes these best. Friends say I'm more
human, while I thank God the form my
illness takes is not *true* mania:
I've never believed I was Jesus,
given all my possessions away,
run up astronomical charges,
awakened, rudely, in a strange place . . .
But *hypomania* was, well, it
was nice; I miss it,

                    then calculate
the price I've paid in depression, of
two kinds: the lifelong malaise I've known
so well; the clinical: living hell,
two years of pain or nothing, numbness—
my Nerves like Tombs—unending Hours
of Lead (outlived)—then Chill—then Stupor—
The only letting go is getting
out, for good, or so it seems.

                    Well then,
let's say I've come to terms, for now, out
of fear. Will another two sane years
give me the nerve to do without this
drug? I am not losing sleep, just some
dark brown and silver-gray fine hairs I'll
continue to sweep (though the parquet
is bare) secretly under the rug.

Nepenthe

Some will have it . . . the Nepenthes of Homer.
Evelyn, Acetaria 14, 1699

On the second anniversary of
my second attempt, a dream came to me:

A locked room in a tallish building, art
nouveau, more boarding school than hospital.
A cubicle—the window was not barred—
empty but for the bed. At dawn a nurse
carries in one heavy plastic capful
of a thick, clear-yellow liquid. Sickly
sweet and hard to get down. At noon she re-
turns with two or three times as much. Or was
it two or three nurses this time? I feel
their hands' pressure, remember something . . .

>   *(Whoever drank this mixture in the wine bowl*
>   *would be incapable of tears that day—*
>   *though he should lose mother and father both . . .)*

something like restraints.
                    The dream was silent.
No one spoke. I woke up gasping, gagging,
staggering down from bed, trying to throw
up that second—lethal?—dose. All the while
I heard, echoing time and time again,
the name of the drug. Without being told:

**NEPENTHE: no pathos: not in the P
DR:** A potion or drug the ancients
used for banishing sorrow and pain, gave
to Helen, in Egypt.

>   *(. . . in Egypt, where the rich plantations grow*
>   *herbs of all kinds, maleficent and healthful . . .)*

                  Coughing, shaking,
not sure where I was, but certain my grief
should not be gone so soon, I moved as one
in a dream. Again: *It was March and cold.*

A dream? A nightmare. Must I relive this
scene? I cannot shake off this undying
memory; recovery depends on
the remembrance of pain.

                              Physicians, once
students of Nature, the nature of man,
you know that remedy, that cure come not
from herbs or chemicals alone. Healing
gods, spare me your anodynes, mere respites
from woe, those forgotten plants, "Nepenthe,
Moly, Amaranth, fadeless blooms, that . . . hide
with thin and rainbow wings the shape of Death."

II

Other Lives

> *Those who translate admit others' lives into their own,*
> *become, in that process, the others they cannot be . . .*
> John Hollander

Why are you writing this book?

As a public service. To declare:
it is best to come back from the dead.
For once in my life to celebrate
and laud my kinship with the living.

What do you mean by that?

I had a calling before: to let
the dead speak through me.

Rilke and Ekelöf?

Yes, chiefly them. And my beloved
Etruscans. Sometimes I feel that way
about Rabbe Enckell: I alone
can rescue him from Finland-Swedish
oblivion, or want to . . .

But about going public, getting
personal—shedding the personae
of your Etruscan Things*—you haven't*
done that in years. Instead, you hid,
perfected the art of hiding, of
wearing masks.

"Not until you permit a poet
a mask does he dare tell the truth . . ."
When I reread *ETs* (my pet name
for that book) back in '84, my
glorious Finnish summer, I cast
it aside, understood, at last, what
a living poet I translate meant
by "Rika, stop hiding!" But I was
paralyzed, silent. (I started to
write in Swedish, which scared me nearly

to death!) Allowing the dead to speak
through me, I spoke the truth. If not about
them, then always about myself. No
other way seemed possible. Now *I'm*
the dead soul coming back to life.

What has made the difference?

Disgust and fear. Disgust with fear.
A need to make peace with myself
about lots of things, even you.
You are a help. But finally
I must get back, return to blank,
white sheets when you're not around, leaves
I turned over before I turned
to you. Like many authors—just
think of Rilke—I feared "getting
help" would hurt my writing. Hating,
no, despising myself more each
day I could not write.

Will going public hurt?

Perhaps. At first. At worst there'll be
pointing fingers: "I didn't know
she was crazy!" or "I knew it
all along!" I have considered
fictionalizing the account.
But this is me: intelligent
Brooklynite-Yalie, translator,
poet, compulsive correspondent,
mother of none, good friend to all,
who, for no apparent reason,
tries to kill herself, twice.

A draft for an obit?
Would you try again?

Not without doing my homework!
No, I don't think so but can't rule
it out. *"Self-homicide is not*
so naturally a sin that
it may never be otherwise."

(Donne's *Biathanatos*.) I still
cherish the right to take one's own
life but hope never to want to
again: to study the clock and
look for signs, to stand and watch trains
go by, to have but one steady,
incessant, circular thought in
my mind. I would seek help, not hide.

What about your professional life?

Wasn't it you who said that in my field
having problems like mine would only
seem to enhance one's reputation?
Joking aside, I fear some will judge
these poems a loathsome spilling of guts
(as part of me still does), ill-conceived
from the very first. And sometimes I
fear falling speechless in the classroom.
So many well-made verses, all those
poems that are merely beautiful, now
leave me cold. It seems, more than ever,
in poetry as in life, I need
the warmth of lives fully lived, journeys
the soul has taken, with or without
the mind. Maybe I've caught up, can leave
the dead behind me, now that I'm back:

**Others I cannot be
have been and will become
without shame or fear
I vow to carry you
with me
always
on this side
of life**

BLACK STONES   IV

You look at me
with waste in your eyes
eyes laid waste
                    I see
lines
retreating—in haste or
slow, definite
                    files

         (isolate, inviolate, we
           need not imagine these wars)

Do not go! This
is not the same
ground, the same
battlefield
              On whose
have you lost? In whose
eyes?

            We share
            no history—only
            this moment
            when feeling
                        streams
            through the eye

BLACK STONES   V

(From One to Another)

Not my blackness
but another's
Not my bleakness

      (Black, bleak, etymologically,
      they are confused: Something chars, turns
      swart, dead black; the fire radiates
      an excess of light, a want of hue,
      dead white; all one in the absence
      of color, all one in the blankness,
      the all-consuming blaze.)

Maybe not toward
death, but in those
depths I know like
the back of my hand

      —Are you suicidal? I ask

      —No, she answers, I don't want death
      but change, to wake up changed, a new
      a different person

      —Change is possible, but slow, can
      not be forced like a lock and still
      leave you intact

      —Still, I want it now, must have it
      now, rise now from . . .

            (I fear for her, for her lack of
            patience, fear what I know despair
            can lead one to. But in her voice
            a tongue of flame is crackling,
            flickering black and white, alive.)

      —Help! If I can't get out, can't make
      myself leave the house, could you come
      by now and then and spend some time?

—Yes, of course

> (I will. I will do all I can
> *and do not want to*, knowing too
> well how little I can do. Why
> is it like this? Why do I want
> to run? resent being leaned on?
> Why can't I extend an open palm
> and guide her through the flames? Each
> hell, I suppose, shines separate,
> blinding, depriving us of sight.)

Not my blackness
but another's
so very much
like my own   What
does one have to
offer but time—
intangible—
and whose?

BLACK STONES   VI

We're strange (some of us)   Not
having been loved enough
demonstrably enough
we are shaken, don't know
what to make of your
Liebeserklärungen
loving phrases uttered
years too late (for whom?)

Since my break my father
states iterates: *I
love you I always have!*
supports me now in
every way he can
So that something of
compassion (*Mitleid*
really) can rise in me
But love—the kind one
heedlessly falls
into—the art of
falling itself?

Calling drunk in the dead
of night to tell me
three years ago you "fell—
fought not to fall madly"
your passion for me (as
you see me) was not so
much shocking as crude
I told you the truth—
albeit slant: When we
met I instantly liked
you, was pained to learn
you were not unattached

Old Friend, Would-be
Paramour, you set me
on a shaky pedestal
leave all your burden
in my hands then tie them
behind my back

27

                        Perhaps
my thoughts are too grave and
what was said has slipped
your mind, "stoned" as you were
(as *you* like to call it)
But now—hands bound—heavy
of heart—weighted—I am
falling (unable to
reach out or grasp)   Don't know
into what or from where
Only that you are not
with me   And this is not
the first time

Escape Attempt

There are no words
There is no why
The maples' pale green big new
leaves resemble nothing
I have seen before

(That sense, first time out of the hospital—
    if only "on pass"—life would be new,
pellucid, changed: I could forget the worst,
    the past, live wholly in the moment.)

"Det som är oavslutat glömmer man inte"
(what is unfinished one does not forget)
Göran Tunström said. Close to three years
have gone by since my stay in Payne Whitney,
the last and best of three dread hospitals.
Still I am haunted, a revival house
of scenes like the one in Lena Cronqvist's
painting,
            Escape Attempt

                Lena is barefoot and not
                in a hospital gown. Are
                they doctors or patients, clad
                in white, looking on? One woman
                shrugs; a second grins under
                heavy black frames. The third, sad,
                arms folded—trapped in white sleeves,
                gazes at Lena; her legs
                face another direction,
                begin to inch down the hall.
                The passageway is sterile,
                lined with closed doors, a single
                barred window shines at the end.
                Lena runs toward her room—thick
                legs fly apart in red slacks—
                her two massive hands grapple
                with door and lock. She looks so
                happy, sure of her way out.
                Is it freedom or safety
                she hopes for, expects?

We all have unfinished business, Göran,
endings come too soon: what we abandon,
leave to others, and what abandons us.
Last fall I met your wife, saw her paintings,
choked tears down; we barely talked about them,
not in her studio, not in your home.
Nor did we mention illness, ECT,
or drugs. All but one of the Sankt Jörgens
paintings had long since been sold. More recent
works stunned me, her palette of Death and Pain.
Impossible to forget them. Were they
unfinished, then? What's alive cannot be
finished.
        To one side of *Escape Attempt*,
attached to the frame's left edge, someone's placed
a small landscape of Lena's; it looks like
a flag in her hand. And still it isn't
finished. Open Lena's door: paints, brushes,
canvas: access to Life. For Life is here.
And at this very moment we vanish
into it. We escape.

Shocking Treatment

It's been four years now since my first attempt—
the one it took me years to own as such,
the one I made in terror, crazed for want
of sleep, on the spur of a moment in
my parents' house. Four years. The statute's time
is more than up. Though I never have been
the litigious type, my conscience exceeds
limitations; speak it must. Think back now:
I was ill; your practice of medicine
nearly killed me, plucked two years from my life.

Your first mistake was to see me at all.
Your second, prescribing the Elavil.
Your third—unseemly, unconscionable—
disregarding the symptoms I divulged:
sleeplessness, electricity streaming
through my arms and legs. Ever my mother's
psychiatrist, you dismissed these both as
minor side effects. To my father you
confess, in retrospect, you'd never dreamt
I might be a *bipolar*, offer to
do a credentials check on whoever
succeeds my shrink. By word and deed you try
my patience, compel me to explore how
much standard error I can grin and bear.

Not long ago, for a friend I surveyed
the *PDR* on Elavil. Reading
PRECAUTIONS gave me quite a shock: *Depressed
patients with manic-depressive illness
may shift to mania.* Old news, but how
those printed words sizzled in basic black
on white! Their message surged from eyes to mind
to heart: A competent psychiatrist
would have that text by heart. I'm no M.D.,
just a bipolar, returned from the dread
antipodes to advise.

Physician,
practitioner of the healing art, swear
this oath: *No doctor is divine.* Human
frailty, no higher authority, defines
everyone. One shattered survivor stands
before you, exalts life's pieces, pardons
herself, goes on, reciting the doctrine
it seems you have neglected all along:
Heal thyself! Soul-searching begins at home.

A Valediction: Forbidding Moving

Good Doctor:

By the time you read this you'll be gone, not
I (New York is still my town), this note my
response: not a suicide, a Dear John.

Were I still as needy as when leaving
the hospital, helpless to write or read,
what I now glibly term "deconstructed,"
would you have dared to leave? After three years
of semi-weekly sessions, you—who helped
me to my feet and watched me start to walk—
are not at the end of the stretch of floor
to catch me if I fall. Today I'm in
one piece, but we are not through.
                                    The truth is
I have lost far more than you. A child
may not, but every patient has the right
to demand that care continue. Wasn't
my mother's incapacity (when ill)
enough for one lifetime? Other shrinks die,
they never move away. Your need to change
your life was—I'm at a loss to say—was
unthinkable. If we were friends, I could
easily carry on; I'm an old hand
at managing distances. . . . You were more
than a friend or parent, asking nothing
for yourself. Nothing but this:
that I graciously let you go.

You know I cling to words in your absence.
Your title hints at ends not yet attained:
In "psychiatrist," *iatros* (healer)
has a somewhat dubious root: akin
to Latin *ira* (ire, wrath), this doctor
may kindle emotion, re-animate,
banking the psyche's flames.
                                    The tears I wept,
when I heard your news, could have slaked a five-
alarm blaze. How ever shall I ignite
my sodden rage? Now you're off, your job half
undone. Not malpractice exactly, this

case of unjust deserts, perhaps just plain
desertion . . . Life's unfair.
                              It's not *your* care
I question; you above all grasp my fear
of other healing hands: Some trembled and
dropped me; some dealt out harsh prescriptions, two
near-fatal blows. With what I know, with all
I've built up, I don't intend to cave in,
never again. At least now I can read,
and if not palms, the writing on the wall:

     Farewell, Good Doctor,
I'm still more sad and scared than furious,
     knowing, without your help,
I should not have written any of this.

                         Vale viatrix!
                         Traveler, farewell

III

Alcun non sia che disperato in preda
si doni al duol, benchè talor n'assaglia
possente si che nostra vita inforsa.

Matthew's Passion

Easter Sunday. *Matthäus Passion* spins.
(Have been revising "A Valediction,"
avoiding writing this.) Can't seem to get
past the first disc's aria, *Buß' und Reu'*.

Yesterday we dyed eggs (it was my
first time). We all laughed while I reddened,
blowing; out oozed the mess. Then you were
too drained for St. Mary's smoky Mass.
The tubes taped to your chest—attached to
a Walkmanlike thing—had kept you from
sleeping; now they deprived your trusting,
greedy eyes of the spectacle: fire
and water and darkness and light, and
Resurrection. I don't know a soul
who burns with life like you. A long list
of "last things" remains for you to do.

Six weeks back you felt fine, felt as well
a twinge of remorse, discussing friends
who share your illness, reveal your fate.
The risk's too great: you can't visit them.
Last weekend you spoke of suicide:
pills you intend to take "when the time
comes." You will need help. I clammed up.
Out of sympathy and in conflict.

The time hasn't come, thank the Lord, we
can go on indulging in horror
films, pick translations apart, bitch when
the mercury shoots above sixty
degrees, diagnose those who shun all
talk of your dying as if Death were
the disease . . .

If only getting down onto my knees
or if writing could work a miracle,
I would not make you well—immortal!
I miss you even now. After we use
up some precious time, I come home and cry.
Matthew, dear friend, the *Passion* ends in tears:

Sleep well   Gather strength   Get to Paris
Complete the Camus   Abide with us
as long as you can   When the time comes
Ruhe sanfte, sanfte ruh'!

BLACK STONES   VII

You will need to die   *(Others, Can wrestle—)*
some day   I pray
not soon   You have good
cause: the disease one
may endure a while
running no risk of
survival   No cure
no vaccine, small hope
for the future (whose—
how soon?)
       You think you
know how to die: first
you'll take an anti-
emetic then two
grams of Nembutal
(don't make my mistake—
the random handful)
You also will need
help: one bodyguard
who will tuck you in
then some poor soul to
come by, discover
your body
       I trust
you will surely know
when the time has come
There's still a question:
Could I be the last
to see you alive
or the first to see
you dead
      and go on?

BLACK STONES   VIII

(And were You lost, I would be—)

Paralyzed in the face
powerless how
to face your death (better
prepared than most)
dissolving at the thought
more frequent now

At thirty-nine you may
be gone   Maybe
before   I who know stop
hoping now in
secret for miracles
remedy cure

Today I am wholly
tears: desire
to keep you here   Who am
I to suggest
any given day should
not be your last?

I have to translate all
your wordless fear
and pain into my own—
again: blankness—
Death's mask devours my face
Like Gretel take

your hand but the woods close
all around and
everything feeds on you
even our
father
          Beyond reason
caution I love

you selfishly   Rush in
where demons have
the floor   We share more than
I'll ever care
to analyze   Time was
writing preserved

anesthetized carried
me somewhere safe
No refuge—here   Only
tears   Sustenance
Colorless substance of
Despair

BLACK STONES   IX

(And I, and Silence)

Again you have withdrawn
into the body of
pain which is killing you
contend by force of will
alone, help—a diamond
hard to accept or own

We are rich, you and I
above all else in friends
who stay on even though
we abandon them   Don't
leave me at a loss now
before you have to go

Giving voice to more than
the physical causes
you to choke, helpless to
spit up the cruelest clot:
the heart in closing has
no more room for love   Is

love so poor it cannot
save anyone? Like stone
the silence of your long
retreats   At this remove
I have no defense but
to write (for fear you won't):

> *Mother come*
> *Mother I'm*
> *dying   Come*
> *let me go*

BLACK STONES   X

(As yet but knock, breathe, shine . . .)

The story about your parents—
that God comes first, stands between
them and you
unconditional love that should spill
be lavished if they knew your truth
dammed by a wall of sin pity shame—
is perverse
My God is supposed to be jealous
yours a God of Love

       —Would you have them give up/put their God aside?
       —Never, that would be asking for their lives

How feebly you lie to yourself
child adored too well
You want nothing more
than what every full-grown
child must fight for:
not the I-love-you-anyway
but the I-love-you-because
want the understanding
that passes their present
tense domestic peace

Part of your family of choice
I share your life's open
secrets, take you as you are
impossible, feel
pressure—the staggering
weight of your vow
of protective silence, love
you anyway and because
of this intend to batter
blow and burn until I break
through *your* wall
temper a hardened heart
and make it mild

On Lithium

I was poisoned, *intoxicated*
a medical text would say, picking
mushrooms in the Swedish woods one day,
late September 1988.
Black ones were scarce; we searched, we scoured.
When a carpet of trumpets with flame-
yellow stems sounded off, Suzanne knelt,
bobbed, gathered dexterously, while each
time I bent down I grew dizzy. Damned
low blood pressure, I thought. Rooted in
marshy soil, I watched her vacuum two
kilos in no time, barely helped tote
the bags to the car. We'd had a late
start and perhaps three cups of coffee
between our breakfast and picnic lunch.
(We hadn't been *sampling* the mushrooms,
and we'd shared dinner the night before.)
De-hy-dra-tion, I stammered, stumbling
out of the car. Who thinks about sweat
or thirst when it's fifty degrees? Once
I'd surmised my lithium level
(not my mood) had swung up to a peak,
far from home and shrink, in the coming
weeks I swigged tanks of water each day.

Blood tests in New York confirmed the self-
diagnosis: high time to lower
the dosage. But why, after two years,
suddenly, why? —Don't know, said my shrink,
not contesting the notion that I
now had come home at last. Three months back,
returned from a trip, I'd felt my old
—not my former—self. (We all have
traits we're glad to leave behind.) Jetlagged,
my body had caught up with my mind.

On two capsules daily both thirst and
hand tremor vanished. My hair hasn't
filled in, the scalp bumps diminished by
vile-smelling selenium and tar
shampoos (recommended by Göran
and Matthew); a Persian rug covers
a patch of oak parquet. It seems I've
adapted.
   —Maybe someday I can
do without lithium carbonate?

—We'll see about that. Why tempt fate?

Home, evidently, is not home free.

Does this still grate? I write with music,
have no visions of infants crawling
on rug or floor. . . . Twice resurrected,
once detoxified, now delivered
from a mushrooming fear of illness
(my own as well as my mother's), I'd
say it's clear: that part of myself worth
celebrating came to life this year.

White Stone

Now love
    a white stone
        falls
to me
        First it swerves
            from afar
then lands
        briefly
            here
Comes with a glance
            a gaze
        (describable, not translatable)
                life-worn and open
My own
        answering
            questioning
                also open

I live in that meeting
            of eyes
                more fully
myself
        from moment
            to movement
In that crossing
        of currents equally
                forceful
streaming
        from opposite
            directions

(I had almost forgotten—no—
I've never known this before)

Time was short
                We spin
                        six hours apart
Our eyes ask
                were we dreaming?
                                rotate
in REM sleep
                It was all
                        impossible
Real
        For once Time
                        need not heal
but simply
                tell
                And will

BLACK STONES   XI

(Flight)

You for whom language is the cutting edge—
a lesion in your throat
Even if treated it will swell
Which is more hellish
starvation or speechlessness?

I wish I'd brought less somber tapes
on this long flight
Pärt's *Stabat Mater* stands
in my ears for you
Wherever I go, everything speaks
of you, is you

Three nights ago: near-perfect
thin-crust pizza, talk of trees
New England Halloweens or
you and Jean on either side
of me (human training wheels)
in the rink in Central Park,
the cocoa you'll make when I'm
back—not chalky or sickly
sweet, one marshmallow in each
cup will yield up its sweetness
to the dark

You must not die
now or ever
it is too soon
Last night on the phone
your parting words
were *Live live live*

I write this *here*
not in a letter
because the pain—
the long future

we will not share—
is too deep, too raw
That I have known you well
now only for one year

I must stop These
tears will explode
my eardrums if
I don't grab hold
                    Matthew
I vow to live
and write for us both

Love

Into the void lovers toss looks thoughts
declarations, imagining these
will be welcomed wholly without
confusion or hesitation
He pleads: *Love, touch alone preserves*
She argues: *Love endures distance*
       (How near can we come in love, out of
       love, how much can be given?)

Longing, he goes too far, hammers out
of her a frieze, a series of scenes
fixed in his memory And though
she wants love to grow to unfold
open steadily, in her it snaps
shut, forced by his memory
       (How far will we go for love, out
       of love, how much can be taken?)

What has gone wrong? Was it untrue? He
mouths the questions *Where has love gone? Will
it return?* His heart holds answers:
Some mistake No God knows Let's hope
He repeats *But I love I miss*
I want . . . will survive without her
       (How long can we wait, out of love, for
       love's return, how long be patient?)

Someone I love is leaving, she writes,
I bid him farewell, a good journey
Someone I love is dying, I can't
say goodbye though the time is coming
How much room do we have for love
just how large is our heart-space?
       (How many can it hold at once
       with no prospect of solace?)
I loved you, I love you still, perhaps
less surely Your words sound the burden
of need: *Will you take care of me?*
Once again in the face of loss
I ask that same question and pray
       your grasp may exceed your reach:
       you will know how to hold me

BLACK STONES   XII

(Care)

The ill can tyrannize
Needing care demanding
care protesting they don't
want it   Some in despair
would sooner die than ask

(I know this well: Once I
pulled threats like ropes around
the throats of those closest
to me   Ask myself still:
*Why did they not flee? What
binds us—love or duty?*)

Helpless irate mostly
oblivious they clutch
and flail all but consume
us   Seizing control through
what they can withhold—
a word a look a kiss
Only a mother's love
survives this

        And we
attend them trembling
and blind uncertain how
much to do when not to

Love that adheres that clings
in the end disables
the sick and the well
Not an abandoning
this letting go

            Past love's
calling care is *lament
grief sorrow*

For Jean

When you take care
your life is clear:
You give up all
you call your life
to ease the end
of another's
Your body for
his—trusting that
yours will endure

Why doesn't count
not now   This is
time out for you
time's end for him
The trivial
falls away   The
essentials
stay: dignity
steadfastness grace

I who also
care admire your
strength (*Strength?* you ask)
not with envy
but hope, stand by
keep watch fill in
I care for you
as well as him
don't want to see

you break   There's no
where else you want
to be, no one
else you care to
see twenty-four
hours a day   You
count pills, coax him
to eat, straighten
the pillows, run

a bath, put on
a latex glove
apply what soothes—
things I can't do
Squeamish, I excel
at questions thoughts
not blood and guts
Last summer a
dear friend wrote me:

> I'm learning, as I nurse
> my father that the worst
> would be protection from
> death's reality. Shit
> and phlegm (now my daily
> medium) have everything
> to do with our shared
> living and dying.
> We are not angelic
> intelligences. . . .
> I'm grateful too—losing
> terror, learning to live
> with grief. The rewards of
> having physical contact
> with approaching death.

I have minced her
words to make them
palatable
To praise simple
actions, human
and possible
I hope someday
to be able
to act as well

as beautifully
In the meantime
know that I care
Know you are in
my heart in more
than metaphor

Life: It Must Suffice Us

On the fourth anniversary of my second
attempt, no dream came to me. Reality
was worse. One dear friend in one hospital:
cancer—inoperable, incurable.
Another in another: tests, procedures, more
sanctioned pills each day than all I swallowed
trying to kill myself.
                    So this is life:
not growth but growths, lesions, metastases,
blood drawn or transfused, diseases so dread
initials replace their names, teams of doctors
unskilled at pronouncing dooms, and treatments—
sulfa, salves, chemotherapy—and words:
prolong, percentile, risk, and *chance*, but never
a mention of *quality*. The best attention
money can buy secures no purchase on
quality of life.

For many days, in shock, I wept and wept,
then flew from bed to bed. How much longer
will they be there? How much time do they have?
What can I do to ease their pain, their fear?
Flowers, the paper, a stuffed polar bear,
just sitting around. Music, yes, and texts: Bach
for the one and Beckett for the other.

Death from AIDS—the many times it comes near, cruel
episodes: the sufferer knocking, knocking
at Death's door and being shut out—I'm getting
used to. Over and over, I've seen Matt age,
turn centenarian, grow younger with rage
and will. For him, dying is not a bad idea.
He has my blessing; may it suffice him.

But Simone—her son, now ten, the first child
I watched grow—for her to die within the year,
how to inure oneself to that? To lose
a friendship I expected to go on for . . .
forever. O, my Sephardic sister, who
else will approve the shades of my lipstick,

the tints and cuts of my hair? Who sing *Dayyenu*
at my family's Seder? Next year—**NEXT YEAR
IN JERUSALEM**—she may be buried
in Israel. We met a year after her father's
death, days before she left for the unveiling.
Soon I may close that frame. And the canvas
we have stretched over thirteen years will serve
as a sheet to cover a mirror.

What purpose is served, watching your young friends die?
I will survive; all thoughts of suicide are
for them—ways out of pain; such fears for myself
have vanished. This passage seems practice, a crash
course, abrupt preparation for other deaths:
my parents', my sisters', my own. I will quit
smoking, steer bodily through straits that my mind
for years has known:

> Death is the *side of life* that is turned away from us . . .
> *there is neither a here nor a beyond, but the great unity* . . .

These words, Rilke's words, are beautiful. Still,
they do not console.

                    Death and death and death,
I thought I knew it, having courted my own;
I thought I knew it when others died, but I
was wrong. Death: what the world in its career
turns and turns and turns away from. No one
spoke of this to me when I was twenty.
And if there have been no words, no tropes for
such occasions before, I must find them now.

We wake, we breathe, we live; we have no choice.
This is the sting of life. The sting of loss.
We cannot accept death. We grow accustomed to
its inevitability (flowers or grass)
in the abstract. Our own friends' deaths are dark spots
and scars on our bodies; we forget how they got there,
consider them harmless, unless they grow:
This one on my right hand I will name Matthew;
this one over my heart I will name Simone.

BLACK STONES   XIII

(As light)

I keep losing them
They die away from
me
     First they enter
their illnesses (no
fault in this—for them
there is nowhere else)
Outside I can't find
them break into their
suffering   My own
pain an orbit a
distant parallel
I remember them
well   An act of will

Then they move away:
Derech Hashalom
Denver—equally
far   Going before
they've gone   Easier
no? not having to
witness   (What does *end*
mean?)   Distance—blessing
or curse—arrives
                    Where
are they?   Have I put
them aside away
let myself be moved
by the stream of the
living?   I'm losing

weight   Another act
of will   For I want
to be so light so
immaterial

I will rise follow
wherever they go
gently hold them in
an embrace
                    as light

as sunlight on skin

BLACK STONES   XIV

(Past tense)

It's over   You're
over   You died
here   In the end
you could not did
not want to go
Your corpse alone
flew to Denver
I did not see
you that last week:
briefly vital
then finally
sunken holding
your mother's and
your sister's hands
saying *Don't leave*

When you left I
was bleeding had
cut my hand on
a jagged tin
felt nothing mind
empty body
numb yet somehow
aware   Pouring
rain New Haven
Elisabeth
turning seven:
Gremlins 2, I
couldn't watch the
gory bits   She
could   You would have
loved this teased me
mercilessly

Hardest of all:
letting the small
things go   One day
in St. Luke's you
asked me to turn
away from you

the near-naked
body I'd held
cradled lifted
from bed to chair
days before —*You're*
squeamish, Rika
—*Matthew, I am*
beyond that now
Holding you help-
less in great pain
was (my mind was
wordless then) was
sacramental

Was and was   The
past tense is hard
to use   You are
under the earth
wearing your French
green linen suit
The glossy black
circles of your
eyeglass frames glare
toward the lid of
not quite the plain
pine coffin you
wanted
            I want
to respect your
wishes honor
your memory
will not forget
the order you
gave me on my
last birthday and
again when once
I had to leave:
Rika, dear friend,
live and live and live!

IV

On Lithium

Poison-wise but pound-foolish. What did
my shrink say? *Volumetrically, you
have undergone a change.* Forced now by
what I won't swallow to ruminate
a theme that draws me like a salt lick,
essential bait.
   At minus twenty-
four, shrinking still, staying with Margaret
on sweltering Capitol Hill—she
had gained thirty pounds in six months of
pregnancy—around Independence
Day, 1990, I was listless,
nauseated, sleeping afternoons
(something I don't do). Matt gone less than
two weeks, Simone not even one.
      Air
pressure changes? Empathy? Escape?
A furlough from the life-and-death hot-
line? The shock to my body, shunted
repeatedly from the sun's ninety-
odd to each dwelling's rough sixty-eight
degrees? All of these numbers combined?

Like the nausea, vague but nagging,
a suspicion lurked. My lithium
level *was* up—.8 instead of
.6—not dangerous (my shrink had
me check it twice) just enough to make
me sick. Now I'm on half of what I
took four years ago. More pounds are off,
and, save the water jug I always
tote, I travel light. This time the need
to reduce my maintenance dose seemed
wholly physiological. But
was it? And will I ever know? My
mind and body are not separate.

Come to terms, had you, for *life*? Well, whose?
Not in my shoes, a psychiatrist
in a D.C. hospital ward said
I should regard my mental illness
as I would a broken leg. *You have
made your bed, and lie in it you must.*
(My words.) Her trope was remedial
temporarily. No more depressed
and never a maniac, I can't
deem the whole nature of my temper
and my sanity dependent on
450 mgs of matter
taken at bedtime.

Bipolar? Labels are useful when
their glue adheres. I did for thirty-
one years without one. Downcast at times,
despondent, perhaps genetically
plagued by a strain of the family
illness. *Lithium*, my mind prods, *is
also used as a prophylaxis
against other kinds of recurrent
depression. Remember what you stand
to lose.*
      Two years of my life, during
which forty pounds of added flesh were
all I could bear to hold close . . .

More than mind matters. *Normal life* (read
unconsciousness or *neglect*) simply
deadens brainchildren to warning signs,
tinkering with our homeostats;
they *go off* all right, but we're deaf to
alarms. Swelled heads will muffle, stifle
almost anything.
      I know I've changed
and likely will again. Addicted
now to the force of sustained control,
I have no craving for the wildest
episode of hypomania.
In years to come, my thyroid gland or
kidneys may exhort: *It stings! Take your
last lick of that salt!* Or I might want
a child of my own flesh so much that
the desire will counterpoise the risk.

Questions remain after my nightly
swallow—two down, bottle inverted
to show I've had my fill, my measure:
On lithium now and forever?
The dose split over and over, in
halves, quarters, eighths, subatomically?
Lithium carbonate (verbatim,
more or less, from the dictionary)
—crystalline, powdery, white—is used
chiefly in the glass and ceramic
industries . . . Still no *in vitro* tests
to confirm biological need?
My body as retort? Rika, that
will be enough! Such terms are neither
fair nor right. Come blue skies or brainstorms,
it's back to the lab, to the ceaseless
experiment, better known as *life*.

Departures

In memory of Moris Fogelhut (1888?–1970)

1. *Ich habe Tote, . . .*

The broken chair of wood, of mahogany—the one that used
to be his, with cushions of fluffy gold brocade, changed
by his daughter, later, for something flatter, more
American in pattern, almost colonial, even as he lived
with us in the house; the small oak table with liberty
bells cut out of its sides, two shelves for books or whatnots;
the paired twin beds with bells in bas-relief on the headboards,
missing, burned long ago in another room;
the four-poster he died in, naturally, now mine:
these furnishings rebuke my heedlessness: as if I sinned
the day he died—not practicing piano in the morning
before I left. Reproach me—for not having wept enough,
for not learning the siddur, the mahzor, the Torah—
for keeping appointments, customs, never faith.

Because we name our children for the dead, I am "Rika,"
after his only wife. In our albums she is sturdy and
large-breasted, almost stern. The name, as given to me,
had no meaning. Passed down like a poem conned to rote.
And yet we learn it does mean "limb" in Bulgarian,
"pear blossom" in Japanese, "rich" in Swedish; often
misspelled, and either mispronounced at birth or ever since . . .
What is mine by custom is empty of meaning.
Only a word that I must renew. What was I born to:
Galicia, his *glil-ha-goyim*, turned in for a new land,
when and why forgotten. Short-sighted, my grandfather
might fail to recognize me in the street. But how he'd keep
the Sabbath, how his hands would hold the keys to the temple.
How he would touch the doorposts when he entered or left.

2. . . . *und ich liess . . .*

Why do you live in Sweden?

>   *Because my work is portable.*

Why?

>   *Because I had a lot to leave.*

What do you speak?

>   *Swedish, English, sometimes German.*

What?

>   *I have not said one word in three months.*

Do you feel safe?

>   *Ja visst!*

Do you?

>   *Only in the dark.*

How do you spend your evenings?

>   *Writing, writing many letters, many words.*

How?

>   *I sleep with a strange man every night.*

In your letters you wrote you had many friends.

>   *In my letters I am given to lies.*

In your letters . . .

>   *Yes I **had** friends; all are dead to me.*

Would you prefer that we did not come to see you?

>   *Stay where you are lest you see me as I am.*

Would you prefer . . .

>   *Of course you must come, you are all I have left.*

3. . . . *sie hin*

Leaving, yes. When I returned that day, he was still warm
with death. He had just asked once more for the plain box of pine.
Never having known me as now I am: thinner, full
of languages he had no use for.
He is the old man walking through my head,
a memory scratching like a cane on slate.
Whose was that slogan, *Death will set me free?* Renew,
rejuvenate—words that must expire. If I render them
I do not give them up. These are my words, my landscape,
the peoples I am heir to. All that we have
is not all we possess. We can give twice as much—
like the mirror that upsets us in the morning
consoling us at night. What was it Rilke wrote?

> We have, where we love, only this:
> to release each other, for to hold one another
> comes easily to us, and need not be learned.

To release each other, to widen the freedom
in our poverty we name "love," by giving back,
by returning to what has been freely given.

1974

The Other Life

It is not the work of art you make
It is yourself
Gunnar Ekelöf, "Ex Ponto"

You cannot
enter into any bond and
be free of it
Göran Sonnevi

How was it this time?

Too brief. After seventeen years, more
than a word-hoard unlocks. In four weeks
links—friends present and former loves and
associations—go critical,
unleash a chain reaction that can't
be contained in time. Time enough to
revive the other language, not to
resume the other life.

Why Sweden in the first place?

God knows, the choice was arbitrary.
I was sick of German and tired of
interpreting. At Yale, having dropped
Organic Chem and put all my eggs
in the Literature Basket,
I felt a crack. Gluing mind and soul
together demanded going back
to rote, learning things by heart. Language
study, first of all, means commitment
to rules, keeping oneself within lines,
not reading between them. Call it a
"rage for order." Experiments—like
living abroad—came later.

And you liked living there?

I wouldn't say that, for many years
it was more an ambivalence. I
landed with the language but against
the currents and grain of the culture.
1974: Göteborg

(a port, the second largest city)
was insular, hostile, and anti-
American. There is a term, not
in the lexicons, to describe those
swarthy of complexion or of hair:
svartskallar; it's used for unwanted
immigrants, unwelcome *Gastarbeiter*.
Technically not one of them, I still
belonged nowhere, left the Department
dumbfounded because—except to note
some *ibid* should read *op cit*—no one
spoke in seminars. Inside silence
reigned, outside it poured; trained to speak
my mind, I was becoming a sleeping
Fury. Best to stay home alone, stay
up all night, as Ekelöf prescribed.
Then, at least, the sky, diurnally
skull-gray, went black as my hair; only
then, *"ensam i tysta Natten,"* could
I work calmly, faculties clear.

And yet you returned repeatedly.

I went as a sleepwalker, blindly,
oblivious. A small voice urged: *Face
the silence, contend with intervals
of displacement, loss of your mother
tongue.* I can't say when
                          this laconic,
taciturn people made me their own.
(Perhaps I had reinstated home
away from home.)
                  Without blood ties I'm
still a mystery. From Ekelöf
to Sonnevi, correspondences
have been subjective, arbitrary.

Over lunch years ago (not *gravad
lax* but sushi) here in New York, my
favorite editor asked me, *Rika,
when you speak Swedish or German, are
you a different person?* Something must
have slipped out—I had not yet learned
to hold my tongue—like "Swedes hardly speak
to anyone." Thinking, silently,
Yes, I am, but did not mean to be.

Silent or split?

Keeping silence is a decision
and a tool; self-division is not
wholly within one's control. Only
this last year or so have I felt one
and the same wherever. Surprises
do come:
            Hässelby Strand in August,
guest in an apartment of a friend
of a friend, one whose walls of windows
opened on Mälaren, I would rise
with the sun to see what the lake was
doing. Waves? The shape and texture of
clouds perched closer at high latitude?
Göran and I worked there afternoons.
Where was I? Or was that *who?* A New
Yorker, still? I, ecstatic to be
peripheral, forty minutes from
the suck and whorl of central Stockholm!

Did you go elsewhere?

Oh yes, to pick mushrooms once or twice,
just where is secret, of course. And to
Sigtuna. Nine years past the time I
turned up unannounced—so nervous, three
times I circled the Ekelöf house
before finding it! Ingrid likes to
play the recluse. This day, so it turned
out, was her daughter's birthday. Suzanne,
a scant year older than I, her son
Marcus, thirteen (they live in Aix), Ingrid
about eighty, three generations . . .

You were happy then?

I could not shake Grief, damned flatfoot, blood-
hound from Hell. 1990 goes down
an Inferno year:
            Mary Sandbach—
Strindberg-translator, dear oldest friend
at eighty-nine—was dying. I would
not see her at her daughter's party
in Gamla Stan or out for a stroll

down Kammakargatan. Now she's gone,
died at home in Cambridge this autumn.
I hear her voice, the laugh that puckered
her massively wrinkled face. That she
was old does not make her end hurt less.

Where are you now?

Back in my old stomping grounds, home in
exile—the East River my Black Sea;
both tongues Greek to me, I'll tie the roots,
declare *ex ponto* from the Bridge, Hart's
"harp and altar." (We share a birthday.)
Home at work, at home in pain, making
myself over again:
               The Human
Bridge—her cables and strings of fury
resonate; of flesh, most tenuous
link and briefest span; restless *enjambe-*
ment, unable to set her feet down
invariably on either side.

Where will this lead? Where would I like to
be? I'm not sure the answer is mine.
"Art is deep uncertainty." (That last
word also means "insecurity";
Gunnar, peace.) I will tread softly, soul
and body bound wherever the tide
of my heart's blood, rising and falling,
carries me.

For a Friend

In memory of Simone Abitbol Golby (1946?–1990)

Thirteen years not
time enough   We were
to have (seven
months past your death I
did not know how
many tears I had)
the second half
of our lives to
enjoy ourselves
each other

       Your end
precipitous
pained   Your son will take
his time to grow
Remote now too: a
faraway life—
step-mother and -sibs
a father you
and I knew better
than to trust

Waiting for a bed
you dreamed you came
to an edge   A gorge
an abyss yawned
at your feet   No more
steps to take   Wings
strong wings spread from your
scapulae
      You
would fly farther than
we knew

      Hear me:
Be a miracle
Help . . . as the farthest
sometimes helps:
        in me

For Elisabeth

What do I mean to tell you, you at six,
child not mine, the one child I will have?
Why do I need to write you in this book
of horrors—illness, death? You who dance
through your fevers, ask, at a funeral, if
the dead in their private boxes must wear
clothes, muse afterward: so many old folks,
there must be thousands more underground.
So unlike the child I was at your age.

Am now. With thirty years between us, you
insist that until I have a kid, I'll
be one. . . . By *kid* I guess you mean a state
of mind, of play, a gift for entering
someone else's imagination (yours).
Or is it merely, spoiling godmother
that I am, I rarely scold or forbid
anything but sweets at 10 a.m.?

Elisabeth, I love you, love how you
beg me to stay on longer than I plan,
love the sound of your voice on my phone tape
saying, "Rika, [kiss, kiss, kiss, kiss] when
are you coming next?" Love how your love asks
nothing but that I play.
                              I've missed half of
your birthdays, sick with a sickness I pray you
will never know.
                        Happy child, how old will
you grow before you read this book? I grew
up with my nose in books, my mother's illness
before my shielded but seeing eyes,
the weight of it pressing the life out of
my life, which, as someday you'll learn, I
have tried to take.
                        The gift I would like to
make you (for once not pink doughnuts, heart-shaped
stickers or soap, paper fans, or tiny
dinosaurs) is the hope and the knowledge:

The worst does pass and can be survived.

Summer's child, camp is over. Your mom says
two of your front teeth are loose. My mind's eye
blinks: You are prone on your bed, kicking up
your heels, wearing a bra and god-knows-what
kind of post-punk hairdo, talking for hours
and hours on the phone . . . to me I hope,
planning the trip to Sweden I promised
you at four, or calling to say: "Rika,
I just read that book of yours, you know,
the one with *Hell* in the title. It's alright,
I love you. All right, that is, except for
the poem about me. What made you think I
was so happy?"

          You did. Your joy was
contagious. It was your gift to me.

1989

September '92: Measures

Fats, sweets, thick dairy, eggplant in olive oil
Cigarettes, a pipe, Nicorette, gradually bumming all
Fear of movement, missteps, exertion, injury
These I gave up over two years
somewhat uneasily—smoking died
hard   In their place
Nautilus, acupuncture, NordicTrack, free weights
And in May we began to lower my lithium
slowly   Three months I wept
for the old diagnoses
Bipolar u, my shrink calls me now (meaning "unspecified")
a term of affection, I feel—even if medical   *She* needs
this kind of language
I give up her fear I'll become manic, my own of becoming depressed
the rational desire, at times, not to exist
at this point in history
I give up my father's demand everything be verifiable scientifically
my mother's belief new miseries await us each day
I give up carrying messages
the compulsion to translate
other people's work   Look
at me   I have ceased
hiding   Here
I am

I give up hating my parents, though sometimes I'll scold them
for bringing me into the world
What were you thinking? I ask
I love them despite their blindness for their blindness   Don't know
what else to call this feeling after all these years
That so much of life is ridiculous arbitrary
so many years have been wasted are wasted—inevitably?—time and
again in family after family birth after birth

no matter how much LOVE is assumed or declared There
is so much misery It is so powerful it kills heedlessly
many more than it challenges I have seen this with my own eyes
I have been only one mirror One pair of crazed
eyes—splintered yet intact—returned from the world of glass

If it were mine

        to start again from

                the beginning

to choose the time

        the place

            the life

I would change

        just about everything

                It is not

        So I choose
        to lie down beside
        what was my
        illness   Face to face
        memorize
        its features   Then stand
        up erect
        very relaxed with
        poise with grace
        And walk
        away from it

Epilogue: Dödsdansen

After the Fall

Standing in the midst of my illness
alone. Psychiatrist gone. The work
undone. The incident, the "fall"—deadly,
yes, but hardly suicidal—comes
in disparate forms, whose outlines blur:

There may have been gunshots.
A woman says I jumped.
I sleeprode to the subway stop
called East New York, near where
I grew up (my father says
there the platform rises 50
or 60 feet). To hit the street
where I did, transit police claim
I had to climb over two large
obstacles. Can this be believed?
In the gym when I mount the Gravitron
and the platform hoists me to
the chinning bars, unstable,
my legs shake.

   I recall nothing past
the day before. I couldn't tell I was verging
on mania. Whatever else took place, I lost
control. Whether I fell, jumped, or was
pushed, from iliac crest to acetabulum,
my pelvis broke (a big white pretzel snapping),
as did a bone in the wrist on the same side.
I could have died, but healed, and almost
painlessly. There was, of course, an injury
to my head. The worst harm done was to my
psyche. Psyche, I say, not pride—that comes
before a fall.
   That I am back on
lithium now is quite all right, but how
to see myself the whole of the prior
year? How to look at you now disappeared,
invisible doctor?

Parting

Once I could walk again, I had to know
what had happened to you. Your office tape
had gone six months unchanged. To get your
"covering" doctor to reveal anything
(back in the fall, she was incompetent;
doesn't a pro return an urgent
call in under 48 hours?)
my new psychiatrist had to say I would sue;
myself tell her I dared not presume
she gave a damn whether I lived or died.

You have ovarian cancer.
                        Inside,
something dissolved, allowed me to feel
for you. More like a friend than a doctor?
Close in age, five months into our fifth year
together, we both knew how many deaths
I'd survived. In the end (*What does "End" mean?*)
Death is the side of life *that is turned
away from us.* Where are you? What gives
you the right to turn away before I've
said goodbye?

                 And the fall? you ask.
Whether or not this fall's fall was a leap
to a conclusion Life won't let me make,
there's now a crack, a parting in my life,
a fissure in what I termed my "progress."
To heal it is to get bone knit back to bone.

Which slowly I do (it is hardly
possible to imagine how slowly),
watch the white fibers bridge the dark rift
until solidly my whole skeleton
can bear weight, stand, and bid *Farewell.*

Glossary

A glossary of pharmaceutical and medical terms precedes the more general notes to the poems. The notes also refer to this glossary.

BID: [Latin *bis in die*] twice a day.

bipolar, bipolar disorder: Bipolar Disorder, *DSM-III*, is equivalent to Manic-Depressive Illness in the older *DSM-II* terminology. See Manic-Depressive Illness.

Chlor-Trimeton: (chlorpheniramine) a non–prescription antihistamine.

Dalmane: (flurazepam hydrochloride) a hypnotic agent.

DSM: *Diagnostic and Statistical Manual of Mental Disorders*, published by the American Psychiatric Association. The most recent edition is the fourth, *DSM-IV*, 1994. The *DSM* in use at the time these poems were written was *DSM-III-R*, Third Edition-Revised), 1987.

ECT: electroconvulsive (or electroshock) therapy.

Elavil: (amitriptyline hydrochloride) one of the tricyclic antidepressants [see Tricyclics]. One of the precautions noted for Elavil in the *Physicians' Desk Reference (PDR)* reads as follows: "Depressed patients, particularly those with known manic-depressive illness, may experience a shift to mania or hypomania. In these circumstances the dose of amitriptyline may be reduced or a major tranquilizer . . . administered concurrently."

Halofed: (pseudoephedrine hydrochloride) a generic formulation of the non-prescription nasal decongestant better known under the brand name Sudafed.

Hypomania: a mild mania; the predominant mood of someone in a hypomanic state may be either elevated, expansive, or irritable. [See Manic-Depressive Illness.]

Lithium: Lithium carbonate (Li_2CO_3), a crystalline salt, is a white, light alkaline powder used in the treatment of Manic-Depressive Illness [*q.v.*], not only in the treatment of acute episodes of mania but also as maintenance therapy in preventing both mania and depression.
    Lithium level: Lithium dosage is routinely monitored by the measurement of lithium in the blood serum. The optimal therapeutic blood level for maintenance treatment generally is between 0.5 to 1.0 mEq/liter, 0.6 to 0.8 in most patients.

Intoxication: Lithium toxicity is closely related to serum lithium levels and can occur at doses close to therapeutic levels; thus, it is important for patients on lithium to avoid becoming dehydrated. Among the clinical signs of mild-to-moderate lithium toxicity are diarrhea, nausea, vomiting, drowsiness, lassitude, cognitive impairment, confusion, muscle weakness or twitches, unsteady gait, coarse hand tremor, and blurred vision.

Further notes: The *PDR* lists these among warnings and precautions:

- Fine hand tremor, polyuria and mild thirst may occur during initial therapy . . . and may persist throughout treatment.
- Lithium may cause fetal harm when administered to a pregnant woman.
- Chronic lithium therapy may be associated with diminution of renal concentrating ability, occasionally presenting as nephrogenic diabetes insipidus, with polyuria and polydipsia.

Manic-Depressive Illness: Too often generally assumed to represent only the bipolar form of the illness, manic-depressive illness includes both bipolar and recurrent unipolar forms. It is an episodic disorder with remissions occurring between manic and/or depressive episodes. Further distinctions are made. In *DSM-III-R* terminology:

There are two Bipolar Disorders: Bipolar Disorder, in which there is [*sic*] one or more Manic Episodes (usually with one or more Major Depressive Episodes); and Cyclothymia, in which there are numerous Hypomanic Episodes and numerous periods with depressive symptoms. Disorders with Hypomanic and full Major Depressive Episodes, sometimes referred to as "Bipolar II," are included in the residual category of Bipolar Disorder NOS [Not Otherwise Specified].

DSM-IV gives separate diagnostic categories to Bipolar I Disorder, Bipolar II Disorder (Recurrent Major Depressive Episodes With Hypomanic Episodes), Cyclothymic Disorder, and Bipolar Disorder Not Otherwise Specified.

In the poems that discuss this illness ("For the Record," "Shocking Treatment," the four-part "On Lithium"), I sometimes make a distinction between the "classic" manic depressive (the Bipolar who suffers manic episodes and may alternate between mania and depression) and the "Manic Depressive II" (a Bipolar II, who has had hypomanic and major depressive episodes). In their textbook *Manic-Depressive Illness* (Oxford University Press, 1990), Frederick K. Goodwin and Kay Redfield Jamison offer the following caveat: "Although bipolar II and cyclothymia are often referred to as 'milder forms' of bipolar illness, this notion can be misleading, especially for the bipolar-II patient with serious depressive episodes."

Motrin: a brand of ibuprofen, a nonsteroidal anti-inflammatory agent with analgesic and antipyretic activities, still a prescription drug at the time of the events described in "The Second Time."

Navane: (thiothixene hydrochloride) a psychotropic agent effective in the management of manifestations of psychotic disorders.

Nembutal: (pentobarbital sodium), a barbiturate, a central nervous system depressant used primarily as a sedative hypnotic.

PDR: *Physicians' Desk Reference*, a compendium of prescription drugs, updated annually.

Tricyclics: The tricyclic antidepressants are so named for the three rings in their molecular structures. Those I have been administered, are Elavil (amitriptyline), Pamelor (nortriptyline), and Tofranil (imipramine).

Notes

"The Room"

Phantastes, Eumnestes . . . Alma: Alma, mistress of the House of Temperance, is the Soul; the others, who counsel her, are faculties of memory and imagination; see *The Faerie Queene*, Book II, canto ix.

"For the Record"

See the glossary.

"BLACK STONES"

The title for this sequence of interpolated poems comes from César Vallejo's *"Piedra negra sobre una piedra blanca"* ("Black Stone upon a White Stone"), in which the poet predicts his death in Paris on a rainy Thursday. According to Eugenio Florit (in Stanley Burnshaw's *The Poem Itself*) the Vallejo poem "recalls the ancient practice of memorializing a fortunate event with a white stone, an unfortunate one with a black."

"The Second Time"

See the glossary.

"On Lithium: After One Year . . . After Two"

I owe the title for the multipart "On Lithium" to a Swedish friend, Bengt Andersson (1935–1993). For medical terms, see the glossary.

- *Hufvudstadsbladet* is Helsinki's principal Swedish daily newspaper.
- Rabbe Enckell (1903–1974), Finland-Swedish poet and critic; one of the four great Finland-Swedish modernists.
- Astrid (my AT) is a personal computer, an AST Premium 286.

"Nepenthe"

See the glossary.

"Other Lives"

Enckell: See note to "On Lithium" above.

"Escape Attempt"

Göran Tunström, Swedish novelist and poet, is the husband of the painter Lena Cronqvist. Sankt Jörgens is a psychiatric hospital in Göteborg, where the painter was once a patient; "Escape Attempt" and other hospital paintings date from 1971. Also see the glossary.

"Shocking Treatment"

See the glossary.

The epigraph to part three of this collection comes from Alessandro Striggio's libretto for Monteverdi's *L'Orfeo* and might be rendered as follows: "It is not ours to fall a prey to despair or give ourselves over to grief, even if sometimes the attacks are so forceful that our life is endangered."

"Matthew's Passion"
The first aria of Bach's *Matthäus Passion* (*The Passion According to St. Matthew*) begins with the words *Buß' und Reu'* (penance and remorse). The final chorus of the Passion begins: *Wir setzen uns mit Tränen nieder / Und rufen dir im Grabe zu: / Ruhe sanfte, sanfte ruh'!* (We sit down in tears / and call to Thee in the tomb: / Rest softly, softly rest!) *Ruhe sanfte, sanfte ruh'* (which may also be translated as "Rest peacefully, rest well") is an often repeated refrain.

Camus: Having published a new translation of Camus's *The Stranger*, Matthew Ward was working on translations of *The Plague* and *The Fall*.

"BLACK STONES VII: (Others, Can wrestle—)"
See the glossary.

"On Lithium: The Third Year"
In general, see the glossary.
- Black trumpets: *Craterellus cornucopioides*; trumpets with flame-yellow stems: *Cantharellus lutescens* (formerly placed in the family *Craterellus*).

"BLACK STONES XI: (Flight)"
Arvo Pärt, Estonian composer b. 1935.

"Life: It Must Suffice Us"
During the Seder, a festive meal and commemorative ritual observed on the eve of the first and/or second day of Passover, a narrative of the Exodus is read. One part of the narration is an accretive poem with a responsive refrain: *Dayyenu*, generally translated as "It would have been sufficient" or "It would have been enough," is spoken or sung at the end of each item in a list of things God did for the Jews. For example: "Had He brought us out of Egypt and not supported us for forty years in the wilderness—It would have been enough. Had He supported us for forty years in the wilderness and not given us the Sabbath—It would have been enough. . . ." Traditionally, the final words of the Passover service are "Next year in Jerusalem."

The Rilke quotation is from a letter to his Polish translator Witold Hulewicz.

"BLACK STONES XIII: (As light)"
Derech Hashalom, "Street of Peace," in Dimona, Israel.

"On Lithium: Extended Terms"
See the glossary.

"Departures"
The subtitles of the poem's three sections taken together form the first line of Rilke's "Requiem for a Friend" (written in memory of Paula Modersohn-Becker): "I have Dead, and I let them go." The quotation in section three is from the same poem.

"The Other Life"
The epigraphs, my near-literal translations of lines from Ekelöf and Sonnevi, do not come into English easily or well. The first is from Ekelöf's poem "Ex Ponto," written during the summer of 1953 and published in the 1955 volume entitled *Strountes*. The original Swedish runs: *Det är inte konstverket man gör / Det är sig själv*. The second is from a poem by Göran Sonnevi that was published in the 1967 collection *och nu!* The original Swedish reads: *Du kan inte / ingå någon förening och / bli kvitt den*. "*Förening*" can mean any sort of bond (a chemical bond being foremost in my reading of the line), union, or association—whether political or personal.

"*ensam i tysta Natten*" (alone in the quiet Night): a phrase with which Ekelöf begins four different poems in *Vägvisare till underjorden (Guide to the Underworld)*.

"Art is deep uncertainty . . . insecurity" translates "*Konsten är djup osäkerhet,*" the penultimate line of Ekelöf's poem entitled "*Religionen*" (in *En natt i Otočac*, 1961).

"For a Friend"
The italicized words at the end of this poem are from the conclusion of Rilke's "Requiem for a Friend."

Photograph by Abdullah Bashir Ahmad

Rika Lesser

Author of *Etruscan Things* (Braziller Poetry Series, 1983), Rika Lesser is well-known for her prize-winning translations of poetry: *Guide to the Underworld* by Gunnar Ekelöf (Massachusetts, 1980); *Rilke: Between Roots*, and *A Child Is Not a Knife: Selected Poems of Göran Sonnevi* (Princeton, 1986 and 1993, respectively). She serves on PEN's Executive Board and co-chaired its Translation Committee for six years. Her poems, translations, essays, and reviews have appeared in many magazines including *The American Poetry Review*, *The Nation*, *The New Yorker*, *The New York Times Book Review*, and *The Paris Review*. Born in 1953, an alumna of Yale and Columbia, she resides in Brooklyn Heights. She has begun to write prose on mental health issues.